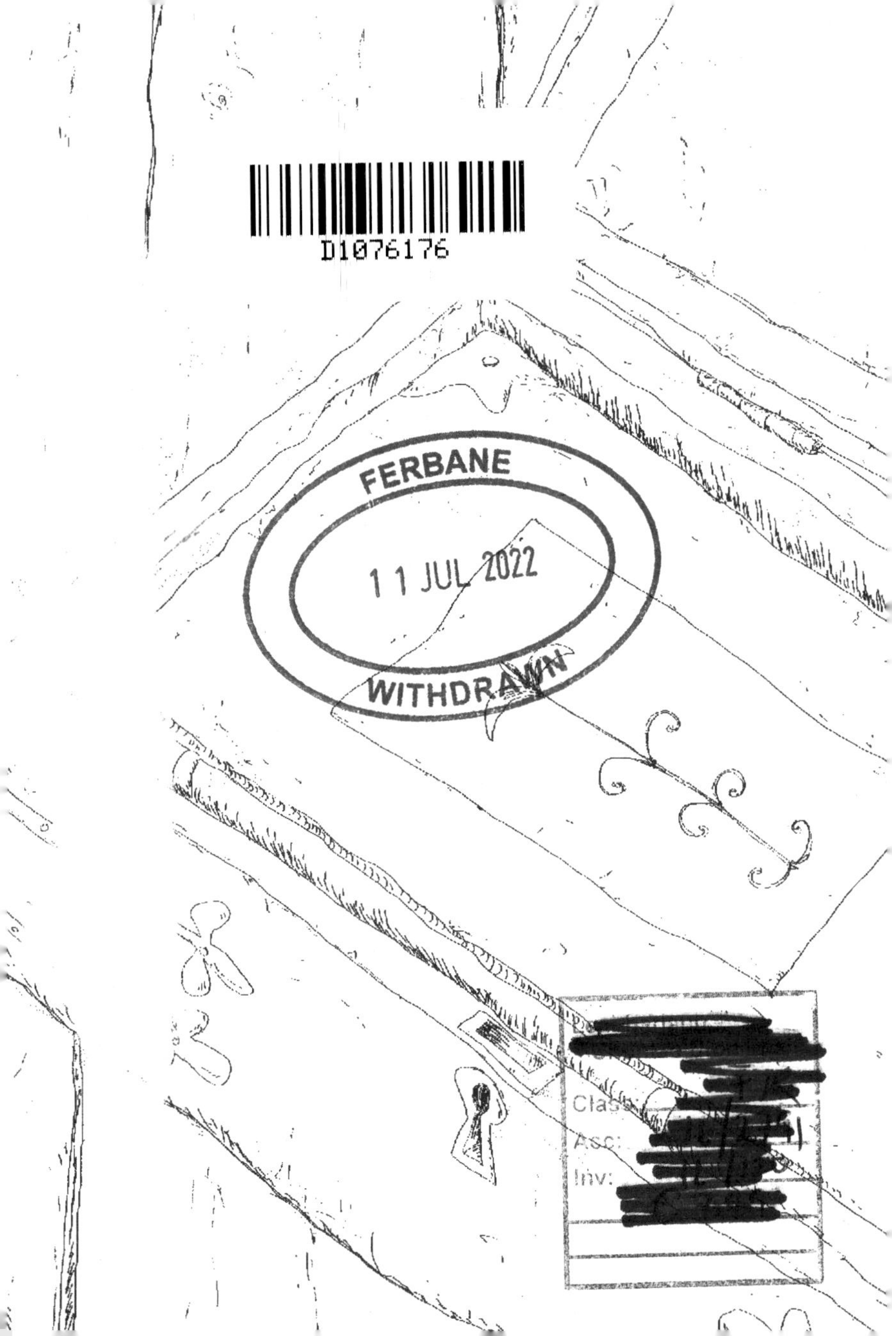

JOE O'BRIEN is an award-winning gardener who lives in Ballyfermot in Dublin. This is his eighth book about the wonderful world of Alfie Green.

DEDICATION

The *Alfie Green* series is dedicated to my son, Ethan, who in his short time in this world taught me to be strong, happy and thankful for the gift of life. Thank you, Ethan, for the inspiration to write.

Alfie Green and the Snowdrop Queen is dedicated to my dear late friend, Paddy Kelly, who loved Christmas.

ACKNOWLEDGEMENTS:

A big thank you to all at The O'Brien Press, to Jean Texier, and, of course, to my readers.

* * *

JEAN TEXIER is a storyboard artist and illustrator. Initially trained in animation, he has worked in the film industry for many years.

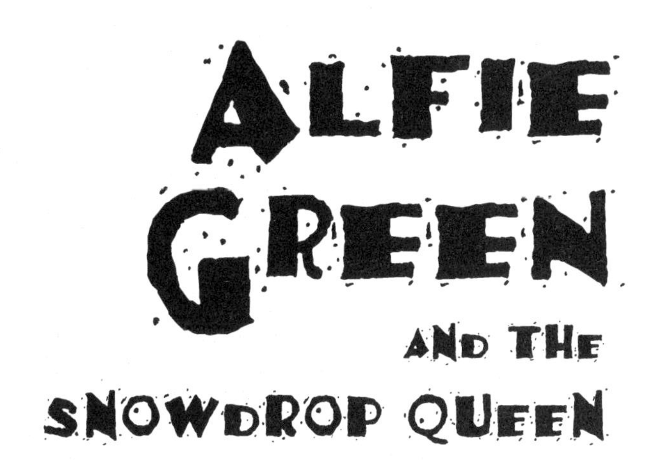

Joe O'Brien

Illustrated by Jean Texier

THE O'BRIEN PRESS
DUBLIN

First published 2008 by The O'Brien Press Ltd.,
12 Terenure Road East, Rathgar, Dublin 6, Ireland.
Tel: +353 1 4923333; Fax: +353 1 4922777
E-mail: books@obrien.ie
Website: www.obrien.ie

ISBN: 978-1-84717-120-7

British Library Cataloguing-in-Publication Data
A catalogue record for this title is available from the British Library

1 2 3 4 5 6 7 8 9 10
08 09 10 11

The O'Brien Press receives
assistance from

Editing, typesetting, layout, design: The O'Brien Press Ltd.
Illustrations: Jean Texier
Printed and bound by ScandBook AB, Sweden

CONTENTS

CHAPTER 1

GRANDAD'S TREE

It was Christmas Eve. Alfie and Fitzer sat on the wall outside Alfie's house, wondering what presents Santa was going to bring them.

'What did you put on your list, Fitzer?' Alfie asked.

'A new bike, a TV for my room, some cool books and a surprise,' Fitzer replied.

'How about you, Alfie?'

'I'll be happy as long as he brings that super fast skateboard I asked for,' Alfie said. 'I really miss the board that Snapper, my fly-trapper, broke.'

'Yeah,' Fitzer grinned, 'that was deadly for quick getaways from Whacker Walsh and his gang.'

Just then, Alfie's front door opened and his granny stepped out, wrapping her scarf around her neck.

Alfie jumped off the wall.

'Got to go, Fitzer.'

'All set, Granny?' he asked.

Alfie waited until his granny had put on her gloves, then they went off, arm-in-arm.

Every Christmas Eve since his grandad died, Alfie took his granny to Budsville Park to visit the Christmas tree that Alfie's grandad had planted many years ago.

'Wow!' gasped Alfie, leaning right back to look up at the top of the tree. 'Isn't Grandad's tree getting enormous?'

'Yes, Alfie,' Granny said proudly. 'It's getting bigger and bigger every year. Your grandad would be very pleased. He loved this Christmas tree so much.'

Alfie heard the Christmas tree give a big sigh, as if Granny's words had made it a little sad.

'But why did he plant his tree here, instead of in our garden?' he asked.

Granny smiled. 'Your grandad wanted this tree to be in a place where all the people of Budsville could come and enjoy it every Christmas.

Maybe they would make a wish. Maybe they would just stand and admire how beautiful it looked when it was covered in snow.'

'But I never saw the tree covered in snow,' Alfie said.

'It did snow, once, when you were a small baby. The tree really looked magical. People came from all over to see it.' Granny looked up at the sky and sighed. 'No sign of snow this year. If your grandad could make magic, I'm sure he would make it snow *every* Christmas.'

'I bet he tried, Granny,' said Alfie.

'Oh, I'm sure he did. But it was still special, because he left a surprise for me under this tree every Christmas morning.'

Alfie noticed tears in Granny's eyes.

'I miss your grandad's surprises, Alfie,' she said.

CHAPTER 2

A Plan

Later that night, when everyone in Budsville was fast asleep, Alfie lay awake. He remembered his granny's words – *If your grandad could make magic, he would make it snow every Christmas.*

Suddenly he sat bolt upright. 'Magic!' he said out loud, 'I know someone who can make magic!'

He threw on some clothes over his pyjamas and crept out of the house. Taking care not to wake Posh and Becks, his sister Lucy's rabbits, he tiptoed through the back garden and into the shed.

He reached under the floorboards and took out the magical book. He placed his hand on the picture of the seed on the first page.

The wise old plant rose up from the book until it towered over Alfie.

'Shouldn't you be in bed, Alfie?' yawned the plant. 'Santa Claus will

be here soon. He won't be happy to find you awake.'

Alfie explained about Grandad's tree and how sad his granny had been.

'Wouldn't it be great if we could make it snow as a surprise for Granny?' Alfie asked hopefully.

'Hmmm,' said the plant, 'There might just be a way to do that.'

He flicked through the magical book until he came to a page that shone so brightly that it lit up the whole shed.

Alfie looked into the book and saw really high, pointy mountains covered in glittering snow. The snow looked as thick and white as his favourite vanilla ice cream.

'Wow!' gasped Alfie. 'It's the most wonderful place ever.'

'Wonderful, but very dangerous,' said the wise old plant. 'Those are the Perilous Peaks of Arcania. There is enough magic there to make snow for the whole world.'

'How?' asked Alfie.

The wise old plant explained that somewhere near the top of the Perilous Peaks was a kingdom of Snowdrop Sprites hidden in a forest of Christmas trees. This kingdom was ruled by the Snowdrop Queen. She had the power to make snow fall anywhere she wished.

'Then that's where I have to go,' Alfie said. He took his crystal orchid from the biscuit tin.'I can get my friends, the tools, to help me.'

'Not so fast!' warned the wise old plant. 'The only way to the top of the Perilous Peaks is through the Perilous Passage. It's far too dangerous for you and the tools.'

Alfie was very upset.

'But if it is the only way to the top, how else am I supposed to get there?'

CHAPTER 3

It's Santa!

Suddenly they heard a thump outside.

Alfie put his crystal orchid on the table and opened the shed door.

'*Ho! Ho! Ho!*'

Santa Claus sprang right up out of Alfie's chimney and landed on the roof of his house.

'It's Santa!' Alfie shouted to the wise old plant.

'Santa? Maybe *he* could give you a lift to the Perilous Peaks?'

'No way,' said Alfie. 'How would he fit his sleigh and all the reindeer through the shed door?'

The wise old plant laughed.

'The same way he fits down your chimney, silly. Now, ask him quickly, before he flies off. Once you're in Arcania, fly north, way beyond Firethorn Valley.'

As Alfie ran out of the shed he heard the plant fold himself back into the book, which closed with a

Just as Santa's sleigh was about to take off, Alfie shouted at the top of his voice.

'SANTA! WAIT!'

'Whoa!' Santa pulled back on the reins. He looked at Alfie in amazement. It was the night before Christmas and there stood a boy all dressed and awake. Why wasn't he tucked up in bed like all the other boys and girls?

'Take me down,' he instructed his reindeer.

With a jingle of bells, the sleigh landed on the grass beside Alfie.

'Why, it's young Alfie Green,' smiled Santa.

Alfie was amazed. 'You know my name!'

'Of course I know your name! I know the names of all the boys and girls who write to me every year.'

He leaned over until his curly white beard almost tickled Alfie's chin.

'Now, Alfie, why aren't you in bed like the other children?'

Alfie Green
Dean Fitzpatrick
Jason Walsh
Conor Houlihan
Jamie O'Brien
Luka Texier
Daniel Bradley
Benjamin Bradley
Killian O'Brien
Alice O'Brien
Katie Brett

CHAPTER 4

Sleigh Ride

Alfie took a deep breath and told Santa about the tree, and about his granny and how he needed snow for Christmas Day.

'Well, it's very nice to hear that you want something for your granny,' Santa was pleased. 'What can I do to help?'

'Will you fly me to the Perilous Peaks in Arcania to see the Snowdrop Queen?'

'If I had time I would,' Santa said, 'but I have so many houses to visit.'

'No problem, Santa! Time stands still in Arcania.'

'Well then, of course I will, if someone will tell me how to get there.'

Alfie explained that they would have to fly into his shed and back out again to the magical world of Arcania.

'Right then, Alfie. Step aboard my sleigh.'

Suddenly Alfie was whooshed up into the Budsville night sky.

Santa pulled on the reins and the reindeer pointed their frosty noses towards the open door of the shed.

'**Aaaaaaaaaaaagh**!' screamed Alfie. 'We're too big for the shed. Pull up, Santa! Pull up!'

‘Ho, Ho, Ho,’ Santa laughed, and Alfie suddenly had the strangest feeling. He was **SHRINKING**!

By the time they reached the shed, Santa, his reindeer, his sleigh and Alfie were small enough to fly around the inside of the shed. Alfie grabbed his crystal orchid as they whizzed by the table.

Then, with another loud 'HO, HO, HO' they blasted out of the shed, getting BIGGER and BIGGER as they climbed into the skies of Arcania.

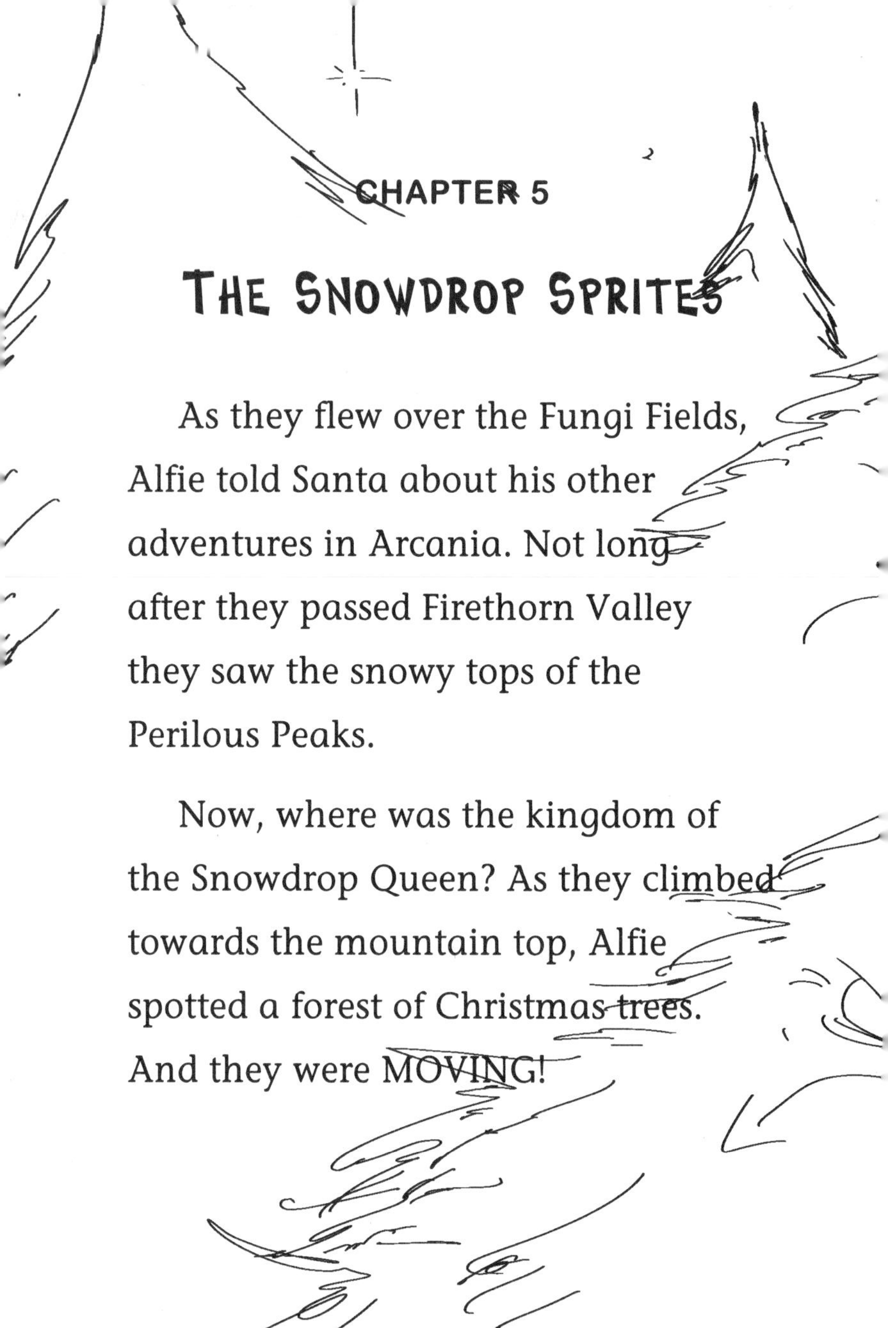

CHAPTER 5

The Snowdrop Sprites

As they flew over the Fungi Fields, Alfie told Santa about his other adventures in Arcania. Not long after they passed Firethorn Valley they saw the snowy tops of the Perilous Peaks.

Now, where was the kingdom of the Snowdrop Queen? As they climbed towards the mountain top, Alfie spotted a forest of Christmas trees. And they were MOVING!

'Down there, Santa, look,' Alfie shouted.

As the army of trees stomped along the Perilous Passage, Alfie noticed that they were covered in splodges of snow.

But it wasn't snow at all! As Santa's sleigh flew closer, they could see hundreds of small creatures clinging to the branches.

They had green hands, green faces, and big, flat green feet. Even their clothes were green.

Everything was green – except for the hair on their heads. That was a big spongy mop of snow white curls.

'They must be the Snowdrop Sprites,' said Alfie.

Santa landed his sleigh on the path ahead of the marching trees. Alfie jumped out and bravely put his hand up to stop them.

'Out of the way, boy,' ordered one of the Snowdrop Sprites. He seemed to be the leader.

Alfie didn't move, and the trees got closer and closer.

He was going to be **SCRUNCHED.**

'HALT!'

Santa stood up in his sleigh. 'Rudolph,' he called, and Rudolph's nose shone bright red like a **STOP** traffic light.

The army came to a sudden halt.

'What do you want?' asked the Snowdrop Sprite leader crossly. 'We're in a hurry.'

'Oh, don't be so mean,' said Santa. 'Alfie just wants to know how to find the Snowdrop Queen.'

There was silence.

'Please, can you take us to your kingdom?' asked Alfie.

'You won't find her there,' the Sprite answered.

'Why not?'

'She's been kidnapped. We're on our way to try to find her.'

CHAPTER 6

The Kidnapped Queen

'Kidnapped? Who would want to kidnap the Queen?' Santa asked.

'Snow Trolls, that's who,' said the Sprite. 'They are being attacked by the Billy-goat Goblins who live in caves below the mountain. They never come up this far because they HATE the snow. But the Trolls raided their food stores and now the Goblins have come up to get their revenge.

'The Trolls are going to force the

Snowdrop Queen to make so much snow that the Goblins will be beaten back.'

'I've never heard of Billy-goat Goblins,' Santa said. 'What exactly are they?'

'They're nasty creatures,' said the Sprite. 'They have the bodies of mountain goats and horrible goblin heads with twisted horns sticking out of their foreheads.'

Alfie didn't like the sound of that. He hopped back onto Santa's sleigh.

'Don't worry, Alfie,' said Santa. 'We'll rescue the Snowdrop Queen.'

That was what Alfie was worried about. He really wanted to surprise Granny on Christmas morning, but Snow Trolls and Billy-goat Goblins seemed like an awful lot of trouble for a bit of snow.

'Now,' Santa said to the Snowdrop Sprite, 'You take care of the Trolls and Goblins and leave the Queen to us.'

Taking hold of the reins, he steered

the reindeer high over the Queen's army as they stomped down the Perilous Passage.

'Look!' Alfie pointed.

A battle was going on beneath them. An army of Billy-goat Goblins charged up the slopes, swinging their rock slings. Speeding towards them came the Trolls. They rolled down the snowy slopes, picking up more and more snow until they crashed into the Goblins as giant snowballs.

'How will the Snow Sprites get through that lot?' Alfie wondered.

'Just keep a lookout for the Queen,' Santa told him.

It was hard to see anything. Everywhere was white. How would he see a white Queen in all that snow?

CHAPTER 7

RESCUE

Just then, something dark caught his eye. On the edge of a large rock that hung over the mountain stood the Snowdrop Queen.

She was beautiful. She wore a long, silky dress of emerald green. On her head was a sparkling crown of pearls. A snarling Snow Troll stood on each side of her, threatening her with their spears.

As Alfie watched, the Queen raised her arms and pointed her hands down the mountain.

A storm of snowflakes flew from her fingers and blew into the faces of the attacking Goblins.

‘Take it down,’ Santa ordered the reindeer.

As Santa’s sleigh flew down towards the icy rock, the Snow Trolls lunged at the Snowdrop Queen.

The terrified Queen stepped back, slipped and fell off the edge of the mountain.

‘Aaaah!’

‘Hang on, Alfie,’ Santa leaned forward and the sleigh swooped down in a steep dive. Alfie could feel the wind rushing past his ears.

Just as the Queen was about to crash to the ground, she was scooped up by the sleigh. She landed safely in the arms of Alfie Green.

The Trolls and Goblins were too busy fighting to see the Queen fly over, but the Snow Sprites gave a huge cheer as their Queen waved at them.

CHAPTER 8

THE HIDDEN KINGDOM

The Queen guided the sleigh through the Perilous Peaks to her hidden kingdom. When they had landed safely, she stepped out of the sleigh and turned to Alfie and Santa.

'How can I thank you for saving me?' she asked. 'Is there anything I can do for you?'

'Go on, Alfie,' Santa encouraged, 'ask the Queen.'

'Please, can you make it snow in Budsville for Christmas morning?' Alfie asked. 'It's a surprise for my granny.'

The Queen picked up a handful of snow and handed it to Alfie.

When Alfie looked down he saw that the snow had changed into beautiful snow white pearls.

'Throw these high into the Budsville sky,' the Snowdrop Queen said, 'and you

will have your snow.'

As Santa's sleigh took off, Alfie grasped his crystal orchid tightly. There was a flash of blinding light and Alfie and Santa were back in the shed.

'Hey!' Santa was impressed. Even the reindeer looked a bit dazed. 'I've never travelled like that before. Now, let's hit the sky.'

Alfie dropped his crystal orchid on the table. Then they flew out of the shed, getting BIGGER and BIGGER as they shot up into the Budsville sky.

As they flew over the park, Alfie flung the magical pearls high in the air. In an instant, snow began to fall upon Budsville.

Santa landed his sleigh for the last time in Alfie's garden.

'Thank you, Santa,' Alfie gave Santa a big hug. 'And don't forget Fitzer's house. It's that one over there.'

'Of course I won't. Merry Christmas, Alfie. Ho, Ho, Ho,' cheered Santa, and his sleigh rose up into the rooftops.

Alfie ran back into the shed and put his crystal orchid into its tin. Before he put the magical book back under the floorboards, he whispered 'It's SNOWING!'

He was sure the wise old plant would hear him.

Then he slipped back into the house and hopped into bed, where he fell fast asleep.

CHAPTER 9

A SPECIAL SURPRISE

On Christmas morning, everyone in Budsville, including Alfie's granny, woke up to a white Christmas.

Alfie looked out of the window and saw old Podge and Mrs Butler having a snowball fight. Even Whacker Walsh seemed to be enjoying himself, throwing snowballs at Fitzer.

Alfie ran down to see what presents were under the tree.

As he was tearing the wrapping

paper from a super-duper racer skateboard, Granny came in.

She had a huge smile on her face.

'Oh, Alfie,' she said, hugging him, 'this is a perfect Christmas. The tree looks beautiful in the snow. And you left such a wonderful surprise for me there, just like Grandad used to do.'

She lifted her hand and turned a small glass snow globe upside down. The snowflakes fell around a tiny, twirling Snowdrop Queen.

Alfie Green looked at the globe and then back at his granny.

'Don't thank me, Granny,' he said, with a big grin. 'I think that surprise might be from Santa.'

And from somewhere far, far away, he thought he heard a faint 'Ho, Ho, Ho'.

READ ALFIE'S OTHER GREAT ADVENTURES IN:

PRAISE FOR THE

ALFIE GREEN SERIES

'Gorgeous books, beautifully illustrated.'

Sunday Independent

'A great choice for boys and girls.'

Irish Independent

'Bright, breezy and full of flesh crawling incidents.

Young readers will love this.'

Village

'... engaging, action-packed story. Beautifully produced.'

***Inis* Magazine**

'Best writer ever.' Siobhan Quigley (age 8)

Laois Voice

'*Alfie Green and the Magical Gift* was the best book

I have ever read in my life.' Hannah Meaney (age 7)

Clare People

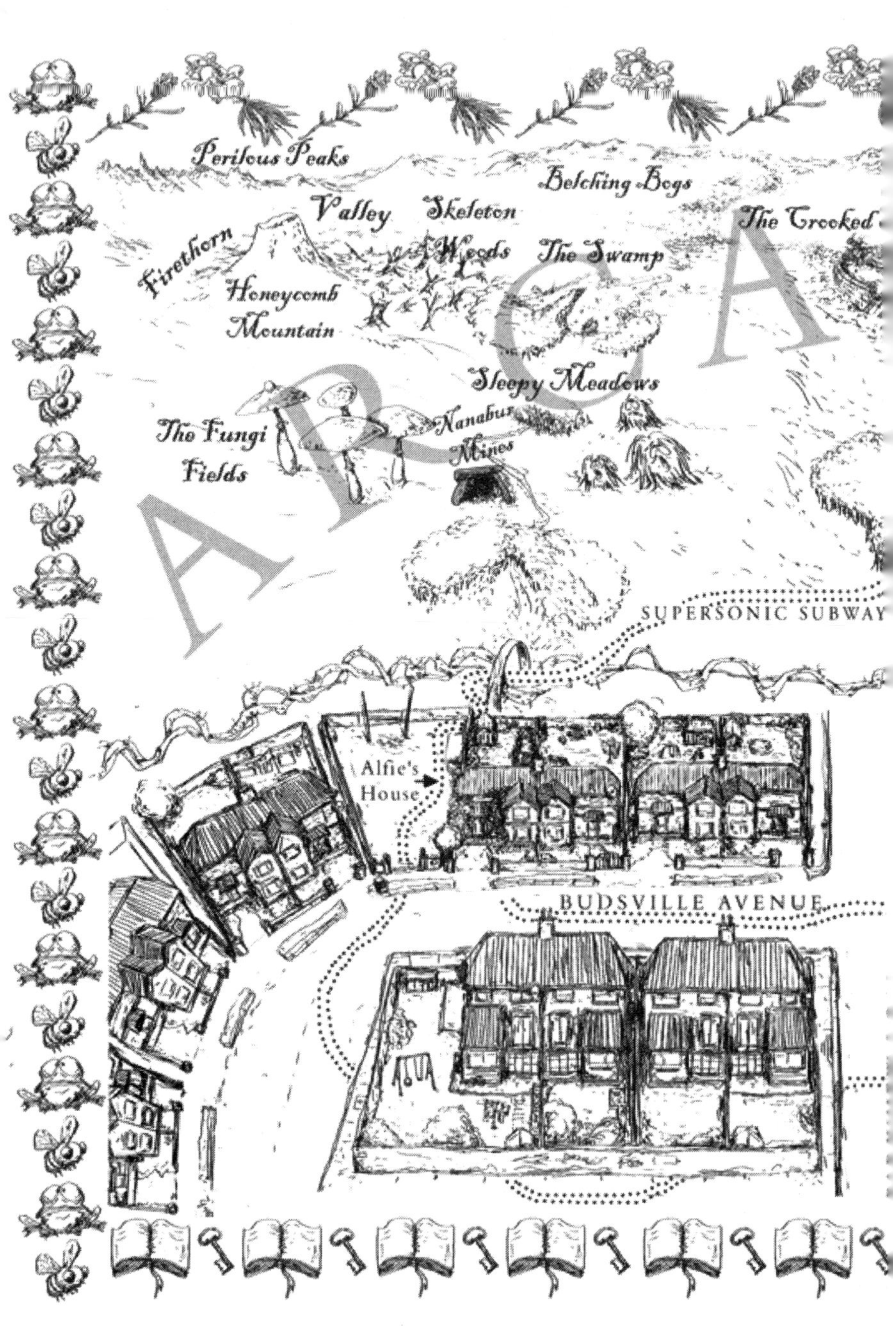
Perilous Peaks
Belching Bogs
Valley
Skeleton
Woods
The Crooked
Firethorn
The Swamp
Honeycomb
Mountain
Sleepy Meadows
The Fungi
Fields
Nanabus
Mines
SUPERSONIC SUBWAY
Alfie's
House
BUDSVILLE AVENUE